®

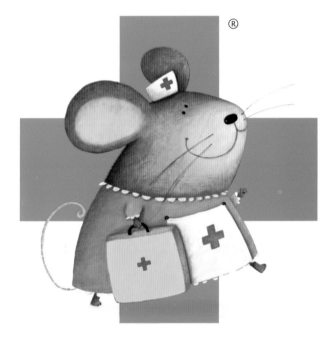

Emo the Elephant

Beyonce the Bear

Nurse Nibbles

Momo the Monkey

George the
Giant Snail

Giselle the Giraffe

Cassie the Cat

Pedro the Penguin

Zoe the Zebra

Sonia the
Snow Rabbit

Chesney the Cheetah

Paul the Python

First published in hardback in 2011 by Hodder Children's Books
This edition published in 2012
Copyright © Get Well Friends Ltd.

WWW.GETWELLFRIENDS.COM

Hodder Children's Books, 338 Euston Road, London, NW1 3BH
Hodder Children's Books Australia, Level 17/207 Kent Street, Sydney, NSW 2000

The right of Kes Gray to be identified as the author and Mary McQuillan as the illustrator
of this Work has been asserted by them in accordance with the Copyright, Designs and Patents Act 1988.

A catalogue record of this book is available from the British Library.

ISBN: 9781 444 90023 1

Hodder Children's Books is a division of Hachette Children's Books
An Hachette UK Company
www.hachette.co.uk

PEDRO
has a Bump!

Kes Gray & Mary McQuillan

Hodder Children's Books

A division of Hachette Children's Books

Hello! I'm Nurse Nibbles, and these are my get well friends.

In my home, I have lots of hospital beds of ALL shapes and sizes.

Which is a good job because poorly animals
come to visit me from ALL over the world!

I've looked after itchy iguanas, croaky crocodiles, sneezy snakes, woozy warthogs, and even rickety reindeers.

Last week a new poorly patient came to see me.
His name was Pedro the penguin and he was feeling
very dizzy indeed!

This is the story of how
Pedro the poorly penguin
bumped his head...

It was a beautiful polar morning.

The sun was shining,
the icebergs were glistening,
and Pedro had decided to
start the day in his favourite way.

With an early morning swim!
Early morning swims can be just the way to
start the day, especially if you are a penguin.

Pedro poured out a lovely big bowl of
Koko Kippers. Penguins who go for early
morning swims know the importance of
a good breakfast.

Pedro cleaned his teeth with his special electric beakbrush. Electric beakbrushes make penguins' teeth as white as snow!

Pedro left his house and skated down the path.

The more he skated, the more excited he felt.
The more excited he felt, the more fun he
wanted to have. Penguins love having fun in
the snow, especially with their friends.

"I'm going SWIMMING!" he shouted,
skidding past the sea lions.

"I'm going DIVING!" he shouted,
throwing a snowball at Alan the albatross.

"COME AND WATCH ME!" he whooped, leap-frogging over the walruses.

"We'd love to!" smiled his friends. After all,
Pedro had been taught to dive by his father,
the best high-board diver in the land.

The sea lions, the walruses and
Alan the albatross walked with Pedro,
throwing snowballs along the way.

"What kind of dive will you do?" they asked,
as Pedro approached the sea.

"MY BEST
DIVE EVER!"
boasted Pedro.

Pedro arrived at the sea and got ready to dive in, just like his father had taught him.

He remembered to tuck in his tummy.

He remembered to curl his toes
and bend his knees.

He remembered to point his beak at the sky.

He remembered to do
his special botty wiggle
and to leap

high,

high,

high

into the air!

But there was one
very important thing
that Pedro had
forgotten to do...

CRUNCH!

He'd forgotten to break
the ice before diving in!

OUCH!

No wonder Pedro was feeling so dizzy!

Never mind, the good news is, just like high-diving penguins, bumps go up and bumps go down!

Pedro did remember to get plenty of rest.
He did remember to take his medicine.
And you'll be very pleased to know
that Pedro the poorly penguin did
get better in...

... THE END!

Emo the Elephant

Beyonce the Bear

Nurse Nibbles

George the
Giant Snail

Momo the Monkey

Giselle the Giraffe

Cassie the Cat

Pedro the Penguin

Zoe the Zebra

Chesney the Cheetah

Sonia the
Snow Rabbit

Paul the Python